T0349402

THE DREAMING GOURD

the Dreaming Gourd

Victoria Long Mowrer

Top Reads Publishing, LLC

Vista, California

ISBN: 978-1-970107-44-9 (hardcover)
ISBN: 978-1-970107-46-3 (ebook)

Library of Congress Control Number: 2023916254

The Dreaming Gourd is published by: Top Reads Publishing, LLC, USA

For information please direct emails to:
Teri@topreadspublishing.com

Cover design, book layout and typography: Teri Rider & Associates
Illustrations: Victoria Mowrer

Printed in the United States of America

Dedication

This book is dedicated to my mother,
Dorothy Alice "Dolly" Long Mowrer

To my grandfather, Harry Joseph "Pappy" Long

and to all my ancestors known and unknown

You know those nights?

Those crystal-clear nights when the stars beckon us to gaze into the heavens to delight in their twinkling wonder?

When we heed their call, we are rewarded with the sight of billions of glittering jewels suspended in an infinite pool of inky black.

Such a dazzling sight!

But it was not always this way.

The inhabitants of Earth loved the stars, for not only were they wonderful to gaze and wish upon, they also helped navigate across vast distances and measure the passing of time.

Earth loved her many creatures, and since they so loved the stars, she radiated sparkling sapphire blue, luscious aqua, and rippling shades of emerald light from her vast oceans, immense lakes, and winding rivers into the heavens in appreciation.

In return, the stars beamed as brightly as they could with great pride and admiration for the little blue planet.

~

There is one gathering of seven stars that is recognized by all. Some know it as the Great Bear, others call it the Drinking Gourd, and many know it as the Big Dipper.

On Earth it always points North. It is a very helpful constellation indeed!

Each of the seven stars of the Big Dipper was home to a different goddess, and all seven delighted in the brilliance of the little blue planet glowing up at them.

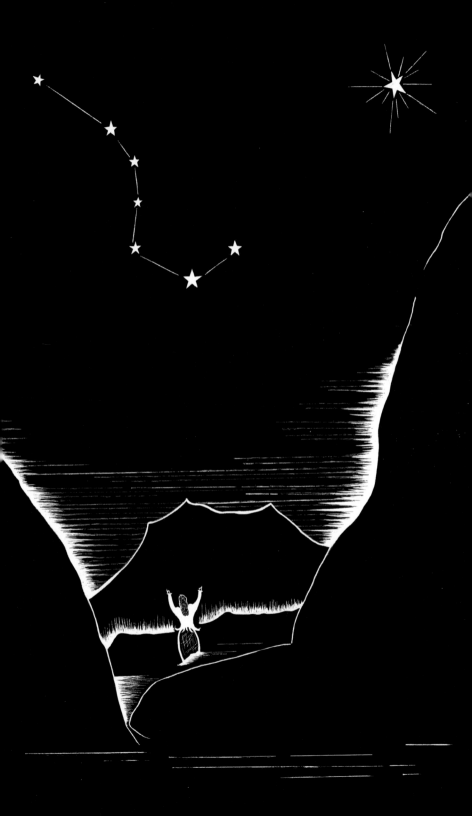

This harmonious exchange of light went on for ages.

But after a time, the inhabitants of Earth no longer looked to the stars.

Not for navigating, not for gazing, and certainly not for wishing upon.

With no one admiring them, the stars lost their desire to shine upon Earth.

And with no stars to look to for guidance and inspiration, Earth and her inhabitants became sad and frightened.

It seemed all connection between the heavenly bodies and Earth had been hopelessly lost.

The light shining from the blue planet became faint and dull, and the stars disappeared from view, leaving the sky in total darkness.

"Something isn't right. We should go to Earth and see if she needs our help!" cried the compassionate goddess from the star near the very tip of the cup of the Big Dipper.

"Ha! What a foolish idea. Earth does not need us, that much is clear," said the practical goddess from the very end of the Big Dipper's handle.

Thus a great debate rang out amongst the seven deities. "If she doesn't need us, then we don't need her either!" snorted the stubborn goddess.

"But how can we be sure? What if she's in trouble?" pleaded the brave goddess.

"We might go all that way for nothing," argued the youngest and most impatient goddess.

"But it could be a great adventure," mused the curious goddess.

"This arguing is getting us nowhere; we should put it to a vote!" suggested the clever goddess.

Each deity cast her vote, and it was decided that the journey would be made.

They would see for themselves why Earth was no longer sharing her light with them.

⁓

As they approached the solar system where Earth lived, they saw short, sharp flashes of green and blue coming from the little planet.

"Earth is TRYING to shine!" exclaimed the compassionate goddess. "She does need our help!"

And with that, she raced ahead to see what could be done.

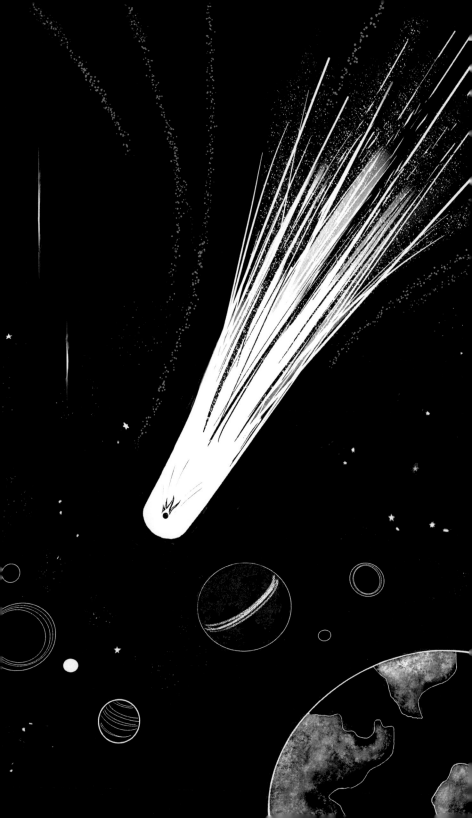

As the others passed within the orbit of Earth's moon, they saw their companion sitting on a cloud high in the Earth's atmosphere.

They thought, "Harumph ... what is she doing just sitting there?!"

Then they heard a soft weeping echo coming from Earth herself.

The group had spent much of the journey bickering and complaining, but once they heard Earth's heartbreaking sobs, a hush fell over them.

The compassionate goddess turned to her fellow deities with tears in her eyes.

"She is worried about the creatures that used to live in harmony on her surface and in her waters.

"The air, once clear and fresh, has grown hazy and foul.

"The trees that protected her skin and cleaned the air are nearly completely gone!

"The waters, once abundant and blue, are now shallow and dirty.

"The land, once teeming with plants and animals of every color and shape, is barren and cracked!"

"But how could this have happened?" cried the curious goddess.

"I will tell you," spoke Earth.

"Over time, my precious creatures stopped gazing at the stars.

"For eons, we had all cared for each other in harmony. They revered me and I was able to provide for their ever-growing needs.

"But, they forgot how to work together to look after my beautiful waters, fertile land, and clear skies.

"The only thing they knew how to do was take and take and take until there was almost nothing left.

"They became frightened, not knowing how to repair the destruction caused by their selfishness, and retreated into the cave dwellings of their ancestors to ensure their survival.

Then Earth let out a cry of deep despair.

"But I need their help!"

The goddesses at once realized that their journey had led them to a mission of great purpose.

They knew it was their duty to help.

"Leave it to ME!" they cried in unison.

Then turning in different directions, they set out to restore harmony to the beautiful blue planet they had come to feel genuine love for.

The clever goddess, who had a way with words, gently plucked a plume from the tail of a generous white swan to make a feather quill.

Then she swept down into the sea and asked a giant octopus for some of its ink.

Back on dry land, she peeled some bark from a young tree and smoothed it with a rock so she could write upon it.

"With these I'll be able to keep a record of everything on Earth and all the steps taken to make things right. Earth's inhabitants will never again forget how to care for her. They will surely honor ME when they see how much I have done for them."

Her choice earned her the name "Scribe."

The stubborn goddess, who was quite resourceful, spotted some shabby-looking sheep and rounded them up.

"If I tend them well, they will give me luxurious wool to weave. I will create blankets for warmth and colorful carpets to sit and rest upon.

"With these items, the cave dwellers will feel comfortable enough to venture outside even in the cold. When they look to the heavens, they will remember how wonderful it is to gaze at the night sky.

"Eventually Earth will shine her colorful light again, and when the stars beam back, the inhabitants will never again forget how important the stars are!

"All will appreciate ME and my skills."

And with that, she claimed the name "Weaver."

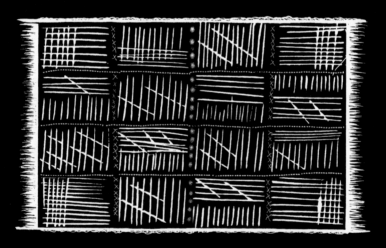

The brave goddess thought about the frightened Earth dwellers huddled in their dark caves, and knew at once what would put things right.

"They won't ever leave those caves if they do not feel safe. I will find the strongest wood and the sharpest stones to create spears and bows and arrows they can use to protect themselves.

"And I will organize great competitions where they can win honors for their sharpened skills.

"They will definitely admire MY cunning and see how powerful I am!"

Quite pleased with this plan, she named herself "Archer."

The practical goddess came upon a patch of sandy, clay loam. This was an exciting discovery!

"The dwellers will need comfortable shelter with window openings to let in light if they are ever to leave their caves. There are so few trees left, but there is plenty of soil to make bricks!

Her imagination went wild with grand visions.

"I shall create the most marvelous dwellings to entice them out of their caves, and this will bring ME much adoration."

She was excited to get to work and chose the name "Builder."

21

22

The curious goddess scanned the land below on her journey to Earth.

As she got closer, she discovered a graceful golden field of wheat ready to be harvested. She wasted no time gathering the grain, then tossing it into the breeze, separating the kernels from the chaff.

"Once the creatures smell the sweet aroma of freshly baked bread, their mouths will water, and they will follow their noses out of their dark, lonely refuges.

"They'll adore ME for the nutritious and delicious loaves I will provide them."

Pleased with herself for her well-thought-out plan, she decided to call herself "Baker."

The compassionate goddess continued to sit for a time in quiet contemplation among the clouds.

She listened to Earth gently weeping when, almost inaudibly, Earth whispered to her, "When they stopped looking to the stars, they lost their ability to dream.

"Dreaming is what helps them create and understand. Their dreams create new things and fix old things.

"Without their dreams, everything is … lost."

The last word echoed out in a gasp.

This shocked the goddess, and hoping to comfort the poor planet, she left her cloud perch and flew down to Earth's surface to devise her way to help.

She glanced this way and that, surveying up and down, until she reached a patch of tall, weedy grass. She laid her hand tenderly upon Earth's surface.

"Everything is going to be OK," she whispered.

In the grass, she came upon several dry, old gourds covered with sooty mold. Something stirred in her heart as she touched them, and, acting on instinct, she gathered the gourds in her arms.

A few of the other goddesses were nearby and began to snicker and giggle.

"What kind of power do you think such ugly things will bring you?" sneered Archer.

"You can't even eat them," laughed Baker.

"What use can they possibly have? Foolish dreamer!" Builder jeered.

Though her feelings were hurt, the goddess walked away with her head held high, the moldy gourds held firmly in her grasp.

The stinging words of the others echoed in her head, but she remembered Earth's whispered lament, and defiantly claimed the name "Dreamer."

From afar, the young, impudent goddess watched the others work on their individual plans. She scoffed at how hard all of their tasks looked as she paced back and forth.

She walked to a rhythm, something she often did to focus her attention. The steady thumping of her feet helped to soothe her, but she was still unable to settle on her own course of action.

She began to sulk, wishing she had stayed on her quiet little star where no one would bother her.

The others, keeping a watchful eye over her, saw her pacing with frustration. Shaking their heads, they also wished she had stayed behind so they could focus on their own tasks.

With resignation, they dubbed her "Impatience."

Dreamer flew back up into the sky and nestled into her favorite cloud. With a gourd in her lap, she pondered her choice.

In some mysterious way, the gourds inspired her. Was it their lovely, curvy shapes that somehow reminded her of herself?

Perhaps it was the rhythmic rattling sound they made when she shook them?

"Well," she mused, "one thing I know for sure is that these musty old gourds contain many, many seeds. And if these seeds are to grow they will need plenty of water."

And so she set off to find a source of deep, clean water that would never run dry.

She discovered so many lovely spots!

There were marvelous sylvan retreats that pleased her eye and relaxed her soul. And she truly loved sitting on the boulders that overlooked the ocean. The rhythm of the waves was calming, and the salty cool breezes on her face felt divine.

But these, though enticing, had to be passed by. They would not provide enough fresh water for her gourds to flourish.

One day in her searching, she came upon a steep, dark chasm. It was a frightening place, even for a goddess. But it somehow drew her onward, and she bravely made her way down, slowly, carefully, to its very bottom.

There she found a rushing stream crashing over rocks and boulders and creating occasional eddies and calm pools.

Dreamer rejoiced with a twirl! She was certain there must be a spring somewhere above. Looking up to the sky with renewed determination, she thought there was just enough daylight left to guide her back to the top.

By the time she reached the surface, the light of day had given way to a moonless, indigo sky. She gathered her gourds around her and quickly fell into a deep, restful sleep.

The next morning she awoke with her senses wide open and she resumed her search. After hunting from sunup to sundown, she heard a delightful sound.

Bubble. Bubble. Bubble.

As she moved toward it and it grew louder, she realized it was the sound of water bubbling to the surface from deep inside the ground.

Suddenly, as if by magic, what she sought for so long was right before her—a spring brimming with water! The pool was surrounded by life. Lovely ferns, luscious reeds, and tumbled rocks fuzzy with bright green moss created a teeming oasis.

She smiled as she gazed into the deep pool of cool, clean, crystal-clear water. Bowing down in reverence, her lips touched its surface and she took a long drink. Her patience had served her well. She had found the water that would assure life!

Dreamer kneeled beside the spring taking in her surroundings.

She found a sharp piece of flint rock near the edge of the water. With the flint, she oh so gently opened a hole in the hard shell of one of the gourds. She reached inside with ease, removing the precious seeds with great care and respect ... for she understood their potential.

With an opening created and the seeds removed, the gourd had transformed into a vessel!

She dipped the vessel into the pool and, with seeds and water-filled gourd in hand, made her way to a parcel of rich, fertile soil nearby, perfect for growing and nurturing young seedlings.

And plant and water the seeds she did with water from her deep, deep well.

In just seven days' time, the seeds sprouted and the vines began to grow. They grew faster and faster with each passing sunset. Soon, they began to twine around one another reaching their long tendrils toward the sun.

Dreamer would sit happily for hours, mesmerized as the slender shoots unfurled before her eyes.

One morning when she awoke from her slumber, she found herself under a beautiful bower of soft, green gourd leaves.

The leaves were huge!

The bower grew larger and denser until it became a complete shelter for her. It protected her from the harsh sun and the fierce blowing winds and provided her a comfortable place to sleep.

Miraculously, the vines bore beautiful flowers. Some were big and yellow and opened during the light of the day. Others were pure white and only showed their faces to the darkness of the night.

One day she heard another exciting sound: Buzz. Buzz. Buzz.

Bees had arrived! This was a very good sign!

Then the moths came to do their work in the secret of the night.

To her delight, the bees and moths helped the flowers turn into tiny green orbs. These would become the very special fruits of the vines.

The pale orbs swelled swiftly, turning into all manner of shapes and sizes!

As the goddess witnessed this marvel, she smiled.

These simple gourd plants would provide everything she needed to help Earth regain glory. The abundant vines could be used to make compost that would insure enough fertile soil to plant over and over again.

But it was the fully grown and dried fruits that provided the real bounty.

She could fashion them into plates and bowls and vessels to store food and water.

They could be used to make special boxes with secure lids to protect precious objects and to create lovely decorative items to please the eye.

There was one that was ideal to use as a ceremonial bowl for the important rituals she would be called on to perform.

She used the fibers inside to make marvelous sponges for taking luxurious baths in her giant gourd tub!

She created flutes, shakers, rattles, and drums to make music to soothe her soul and stir her dancing feet.

All these beautiful and useful things the goddess fashioned, along with dippers for ladling the water of life from her deep, deep well.

These she called her "Drinking Gourds," which also reminded her of her star home so far away.

Finally, she chose a gourd that was perfectly shaped to rest her head upon when she slept.

And this she called her "Dreaming Gourd."

As Dreamer slept, she would dream about the blue planet and all its possibilities. New worlds in the sky above and the sea below appeared in her daydreams and night visions. The fantastic creatures her imagination conjured to inhabit them made her smile.

She dreamed that the glimmer shimmering on the water during the day would once again reflect up to the heavens, and the stars would rejoice.

All these visions made their way through the hard shell of the Dreaming Gourd, embedding themselves in the fertile seeds contained within.

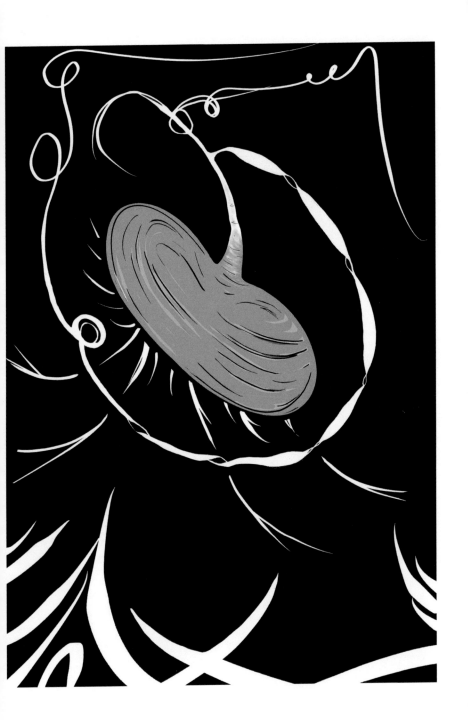

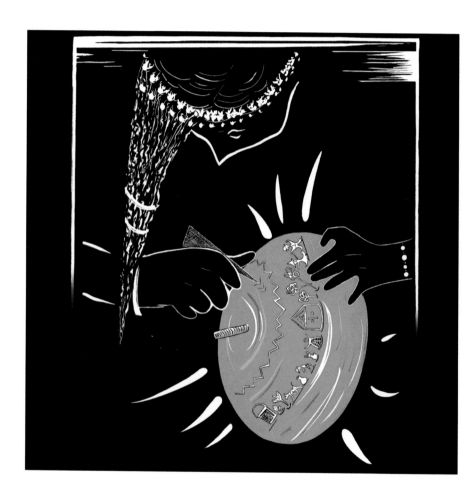

Often Dreamer could be seen sitting in the shady coolness of the lush gourd vine bower that had grown around her.

The other goddesses wondered what she was doing, and they marveled as she spent day after day in a state of patient, focused intention.

What they couldn't see was that she was bent over her Dreaming Gourd, carving images from her dreams into the smooth, hard surface with her flinty stone.

Only Impatience was not impressed in the least.

She thought the goddess in the bower was hopelessly boring.

No rains had fallen since the deities had reached Earth, and the drought, which preceded their arrival, continued to worsen.

Archer, who could no longer find proper wood for the arrows and bows she hoped to present to the frightened cave dwellers, watched anxiously over the others as they struggled with their individual tasks.

Weaver's flock had run out of grass to graze, and their wool was now dull and brittle. She had not been able to weave anything worth presenting to the inhabitants of the caves.

Scribe had to make many tedious trips to retrieve ink from the great octopus any time she thought of something to record on her parchment, and she was running out of fresh tree bark to make parchment from.

Baker had managed only a few meager loaves from the patch of grain, and they were flavorless and hard. No one would be venturing out of their cave for these pitiful breads.

Builder sat with her elbows on her knees and her head in her hands, surrounded by various piles of crumbling, flaky, and formless clumps of dirt. Not a single structure had been built, and she was feeling very sorry for herself.

Impatience, incredibly frustrated about everything, wrapped her arms about herself and tapped her fingers on the tops of her shoulders, cursing this whole pointless trip.

With each passing day, the others became more and more restless while the goddess of the bower seemed calm and unaffected, tucked away in her cool, green haven.

A council was called among the six of them, and after great deliberation it was decided that two would go to the gourd bower to ask Dreamer for help.

They now realized she had chosen very wisely and to the benefit of them all.

Weaver and Scribe were deemed to have the best qualities to make the journey and approach her. They nervously set out bearing gifts: the best of Baker's loaves, a small woven blanket, and notes of apology, written on Scribe's remaining parchment.

When they reached the bower, Dreamer accepted their gifts graciously and patiently listened to their plea.

Scribe began by praising her wisdom, "Your choice has given you an abundance of pure water. Surely you have the goodness of heart to share!"

Weaver followed, "Please forgive all of us for being so rude to you. We're ever so sorry!"

However, Dreamer could see what truly brought them to her was their need for water, not the desire to make amends or to praise her.

She smiled, for this was an opportunity for the others to learn the importance of sharing and cooperation, and uttered the words, "Yes, I will help you."

Weaver and Scribe immediately began to jump with joy, but Dreamer raised her hand to quiet them and continued, "It is not the water from my spring that I will give. You must gather the water you need from the abyss."

Scribe and Weaver shuddered in sudden fear.

They knew the old stories of the earthly abyss and how easily one could fall into its depths and perhaps disappear forever!

The abyss was a deep,

      dark,

           frightening

                mystery.

Weaver and Scribe stood there perplexed as Dreamer handed them a dipper she had fashioned from one of her gourds.

Then she pulled a long, strong piece of vine from her bower.

"Tie this vine around the handle of the gourd to retrieve the water from the pool in the abyss.

"Be very quiet and you will know when the dipper has reached the surface of the pool. There is plenty of water there for all, but with only one gourd, you must learn to patiently share the dipper among yourselves.

"You will see that this humble gourd, something you thought beneath your notice, is capable of a great many things."

With immense hope and gratitude, the dipper, vine, and instructions were taken back to the others.

Although they were still afraid, their need for water drove them, and they all set off to the edge of the abyss, reassuring one another all the while that none of them would fall into its mysterious depths.

All except for one, that is. Our impudent goddess, Impatience.

Wait in line! Ha! Not me. She thought, *I'm not going to wait to take turns like a child! I'll retrieve water from the abyss without anyone's help. Then maybe the others will take ME seriously!*

I can sneak into Dreamer's bower while she sleeps and steal my own gourd!

And off she went to do just that.

However, things did not go quite as easily as young Impatience expected.

Inside the bower, there were no gourds to be found. Dreamer had once again listened to her intuition and had hidden them. The only gourd in sight was the one her head was lying upon as she slept, deeply dreaming visions into her very special pillow.

Hmmm ... Impatience thought. *How can I get that blasted gourd out from under her sleeping head?*

As she crept ever so slowly and quietly toward Dreamer, she saw her solution. There was a feather lying right there on the ground.

She continued to creep closer and closer until she was so near Dreamer's head that she could reach out her arm, the feather in her fingertips, and gently touch the feather to her cheek. One little tickle, then another, and Dreamer turned over in her sleep.

As she shifted, the young goddess slid the Dreaming Gourd out from under her head, replacing it with a smooth stone.

Then away she ran as fast as her feet would carry her!

Disturbed by the unfamiliar hard coolness under her head, Dreamer awoke.

She guessed at once who the unwise intruder must have been. Impatience!

Her normally calm nature gave way to concern. Concern gave way to fear. And fear, as so often happens, gave way to anger.

Her dreams! Stolen! She leaped into action.

She would seek out the thief, reclaim her Dreaming Gourd, and give Impatience a good scolding.

In the meantime, Impatience had reached the edge of the abyss but quickly realized she had no way to lower the stolen gourd into the water.

As she spied the other goddesses through a patch of grasses and shrubs, she saw they were using some sort of rope attached to the handle of their dipper gourd to lower it into the abyss.

Her gourd didn't even have a handle!

Then Impatience thought of Weaver's piles of wool fibers.

She quietly made her way over to Weaver and whispered to her, "If you help me by making a rope, you can come with me and share my water. You will not have to wait in that line with all the others."

With the idea of cooperation fresh in her mind, Weaver obliged Impatience's request and fashioned a rope for her, but declined the offer for a shortcut to get the water.

"I will wait my turn with the others," she said. "It is not wise to arouse anger with your neighbors, especially in times of great duress."

Stupid fool, Impatience thought, snatching the rope from Weaver.

She hurried back to the edge of the abyss, away from the others, determined to attach the rope to the stolen gourd. After a few clumsy attempts, she succeeded.

Excitedly, she lowered the gourd down into the abyss.

Slack in the rope told her it had reached the bottom.

With a smirk of a smile, she pulled the gourd back up into her hands, but the Dreaming Gourd contained not a single drop of water.

In her greedy haste, no attention had been given to important details. Stomping her feet, she realized this gourd did not have an opening!

It was still a pillow and not a vessel! How was she going to crack open the hard shell?

Thump, thump went her feet as she paced about. Boiling with anger, Impatience tried everything.

She threw it on the ground ... it only bounced.

She hit it with a rock ... it ricocheted right off.

Tears of frustration washed down her cheeks as she fell to her knees, pounding the Dreaming Gourd with her bare fists.

Kneeling there on the parched, hard ground, she saw Dreamer hurtling toward her.

"Stop!" Dreamer commanded as she raised her arm straight up in the air, the palm of her hand facing the young goddess.

Impatience froze, then slowly rose from her knees in shame, holding the Dreaming Gourd before her. When she lifted her eyes, she found herself face to face with a very angry and powerful goddess.

"You do not have the knowledge or wisdom to handle an object this potent, and perhaps you never will!

"It is filled with precious visions of all things yet to be and must be handled with great care and reverence."

With this, Dreamer deftly swept the Dreaming Gourd out of Impatience's hands before the thief could utter a single word.

"You are truly impatient!!"

Holding the great gourd in her arms, Dreamer felt a stirring inside her dreaming pillow.

She listened very closely and intently.

There was no question! The time had come for all her incubated dreams to be released from their cocoon.

Guided by her intuition, Dreamer snatched a piece of flint from the ground and struck the gourd in precisely the right spot, cracking it open into two perfect halves.

Awestruck, Dreamer looked at the two halves before her, and her angry frown was slowly replaced with the hint of a smile.

Each half of the gourd contained thousands of seeds filled with her dreams, and each seed had the potential to manifest into something extraordinary.

Dreamer took one half and tossed it gracefully into the abyss, whose waters flowed into the sea.

The other half she flung with great force into the heavens.

She was thrilled!

Their mission to help Earth and her inhabitants would continue on ... and most importantly, her dreams were about to come true!!

The seeds that made their way into the life-giving waters at the bottom of the abyss began to emerge as the plants, animals, bugs, and birds Dreamer had imagined as she slept.

Colorful flowers with fragrances oh so heavenly she could smell them in her dreams!

There were fish that flew and birds that swam.

Creatures with fanciful fur, smooth feathers, leathery shells, and slippery scales.

So many things of wonderous beauty were born and restored.

The seeds flung upward into the heavens became new galaxies filled with stars, planets, and moons.

Earth's skies, dark for so long, now held an abundance of twinkling, shimmering stars filled with new constellations.

Suddenly, a comet burst across the sky, moving north, and the goddesses let out a collective gasp as their home, the Big Dipper, sparkled into view once again.

Impatience stood wide-eyed in stunned silence as the blackness of the heavens became studded with starlight. For the first time in her young immortal life, she realized the immense power of dreaming, and the importance of patience.

And this was the beginning of her wisdom.

Another council was called.

This time it was held in Dreamer's bower at her invitation.

Seeing how the others now revered her beloved gourds, Dreamer first went about bestowing these useful gifts to her neighbors.

To Scribe, she gifted two gourds: a large one that could store a great amount of ink, and a smaller flat one with a stable bottom to serve as an inkwell for her plume.

To Baker she gifted a set of gourds for mixing and storing a variety of delicious ingredients for her breads.

Archer received a very special long and straight gourd to hold her arrows. It was fashioned with a bower vine to secure the quiver onto her back.

To Weaver, she gifted a very large gourd for her sheep to drink from, as well as many bowls to create dyes for her wool from the many flowers and plants that had sprung forth from the Dreaming Gourd.

To Builder, she gifted a massive gourd for mixing water and different kinds of earth into bricks, clay, and grout, as well as a few smaller vessels that would make it easier to get the consistency of each material just right.

And to dear Impatience, Dreamer gifted a great double drum made from the split halves of her Dreaming Gourd, telling her, "Your power comes from within you, and this drum will help you claim it."

Dreamer led the gift-giving with tears in her eyes seeing each goddess admiring the others' gifts, excitedly making plans to help each other.

"Baker, now that my sheep are well fed, they have started giving birth to new lambs. I have extra milk I can share with you to make cheese and butter for your delicious breads!" Weaver exclaimed proudly.

"Builder, I can write instructions for your building materials once you get the formulas just right!" Scribe liked the idea of being able to help her neighbor.

Builder smiled and turned to Baker. "I can build you a great oven now that I have the ability to make better bricks. You'll be able to bake bigger loaves than ever before!"

She was bursting with excitement at the thought of this new project.

"Scribe, you can use some of my bowls to soak tree bark and other fibers to make soft and flexible paper that is easier to write upon," said Baker eager to return the generosity of her friends.

"Archer, I will give you some of my strongest woven string to make your bows" offered Weaver. "That will help your arrows fly farther, faster, and truer!"

Away from the group, Impatience sat admiring her drum. It was the most magnificent gift she had ever received.

She tapped here and there, testing to see what kinds of sounds the drum could produce.

After a few minutes, confident in her power, she began to drum with her fingers, lightly at first and then more powerfully to an ancient, primal rhythm she summoned from deep inside herself.

She felt more at ease than she ever remembered feeling.

In that instant, she became known and celebrated as "Drummer."

Dreamer brought forth her ceremonial bowl and led them in a ritual of celebration for all they had achieved together.

They danced and sang into the wee hours of the star-studded night to the glorious sounds of Dreamer's many gourd instruments, with Drummer at the center, keeping the most wonderful rhythm.

The more music they made and the louder they sang together, the brighter the stars twinkled to celebrate with them!

Their ritual created a cascade of joy from Earth's very core that swept across all the galaxies in the universe.

"Thank you, dear friends!" The blue planet exclaimed as her sparkling sapphire, luscious aqua, and rippling emerald light expanded ever outward into the cosmos once more.

This dazzling show of energy and light was so compelling, it stirred the cave-dwellers, and for the first time in many generations, they emerged from the darkness, blinking up at the billions of stars in the sky with new-found hope in their hearts.

Potential abounds everywhere in every moment.

Be brave and believe.

The End

Which is never really an end—simply a new beginning.

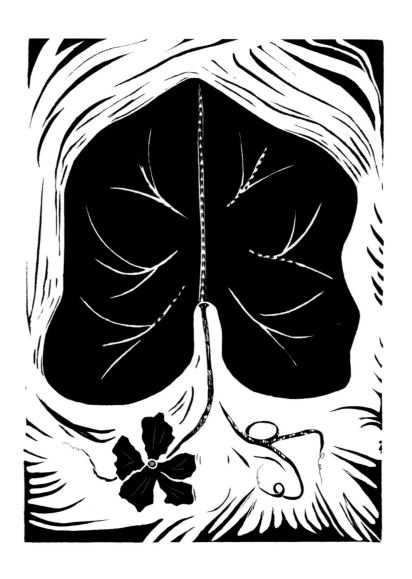

Special Thanks

This story has taken quite a few years to evolve from an oral storytelling to written word. Along the way so many amazing souls that have touched its life and mine.

It had its first glimmer of life simultaneously in Upper Red Hook and Tivoli, NY. I send a thank you to those areas and the many friendships that formed there.

I send a gigantic thank you to the rest of you hither and yon. You know who you are!

A special thanks to those listed below who played a major role in bringing this book into being. The order of appearance is by entry into the journey of *The Dreaming Gourd*.

To Cathy and Gary Wert. You have always been there no matter when and no matter what. I thank my lucky stars for the crossing of our paths.

To Will Lashley. You moved me.

To Dr. John Gerdy. You realized the seeds of potential and watered regularly. And you continue to tend and nurture the ever-expanding garden that is forever grateful for your presence.

To Manny Rivera. You believed and encouraged.

To Tony Rubrecht. You tuned-in to the Universe.

To Jeff Coleman. You shared your time and talent all while providing sustenance on so many levels. You became my personal Big Dipper.

To Teri Rider and Chelsea Robinson. You two are quite an extraordinary mother and daughter team! And a light beam of inspiration for women in the publishing world. Teri, you agreed to be my midwife. My teammate. You believed this book was worth the risk and gave abundantly of your time and efforts during a very long pregnancy! You worked with me, read and reread my words, looked and relooked at all my artworks, held my hand, encouraged, and offered gentle solace as the book baby grew and grew. I could not have done this without you. You are truly amazing. Chelsea, you helped my words fly! There is nothing like an editor that knows how to help a story grow wings. Every time I tossed something new into the fray you handled it with grace, ease and enthusiasm. As you know I adore using … and !!! I likely drove you mad!!!

Victoria Mowrer is a self-taught, multi-disciplinary artist, teller of tales and seeker. She believes beauty in its myriad forms has the power to heal. A passion for exploration, experimentation, and truth-seeking has been with her since childhood. Growing up as an only child on her grandparents' farm in rural Pennsylvania gave her the freedom to seek out adventures in nature that called to her spirit: collecting stones and arrowheads, building life-size snow castles, and molding things out of clay gathered from the banks of the stream and pond in the pine woods nearby. During that time, she witnessed her grandfather being excommunicated from his Mennonite community for purchasing a television.

That experience sparked a wariness of authority and religion and fueled her already inquisitive nature to wonder about complex ideas from a young age.

Always enchanted by the innumerable delights and mediums for creative expression this world has to offer, she's painted, printed, photographed with her Holga, played in a gamelan orchestra, owned a small counter-culture cafe, served as a professional chef, designed gardens, arranged flowers, and sculpted with clay, stone, and gourds. For pioneering a technique of pressing flowers into encaustic art, she was invited to Japan as part of the Nagano Olympics' cultural exchange where she spent two weeks showcasing her art and teaching classes about her techniques. She currently loves singing with a community chorus and as backup for a local blues band where she plays her beloved shekere. She's lived in Puerto Rico, Massachusetts, California, NYC, and Upstate New York. She studied garden design in UK with John Brooks and pebble mosaic in Chicago with Maggie Howarth. Ever in pursuit of adventure, art, stories, and herself, she has found her way back to her roots in Lancaster, PA, where some of her greatest stories are being unearthed as she plows the fields of her past.

The modest gourd has accompanied her as a muse, friend, and guide for more than half her life. And now, she's written an illustrated folk tale about the stars, community, and her beloved gourd companion. What began as an oral recitation atop a giant gourd as part of her one-woman show, "Restlessness and Reverie," has evolved and expanded into a wondrous tale of love, loss, and reclamation. As with everything in her life, the creation of this book carries the heartbeat of her mantra, Be Brave and Believe.

You can learn more about Victoria and *The Dreaming Gourd* by visiting:

www.victorialongmowrer.com
FB: thedreaminggourd
IG: thedreaminggourd

Praise for *The Dreaming Gourd*

"What a beautiful, hopeful story that the seeds of *The Dreaming Gourd* can recreate the earth and the heavens. I will turn to *The Dreaming Gourd* again and again for inspiration and comfort." —Elizabeth Cunningham, author of *My Life as a Prayer*, and *The Maeve Chronicles*

"You've crafted a wonderful story, full of wisdom and hope. A treasure." —Tanis Garber-Shaw

"I think everyone should not only read it but re-read it often to help stay mindful of our actions and what's important. What a beautiful gift you've given the world." —Tina Riley

"Your drawings are so wonderful and the content so relevant!" —K King

"The book imagines the potential/projected devastation that climate change will have on our planet. This serious subject is dealt with in a sensitive, often playful, way. The characters in the book are compassionate, colorful, zany and possess the ability to bring light into the ever-darkening environmental atmosphere that climate change has brought upon us earthlings." — Geraldine WuShanley